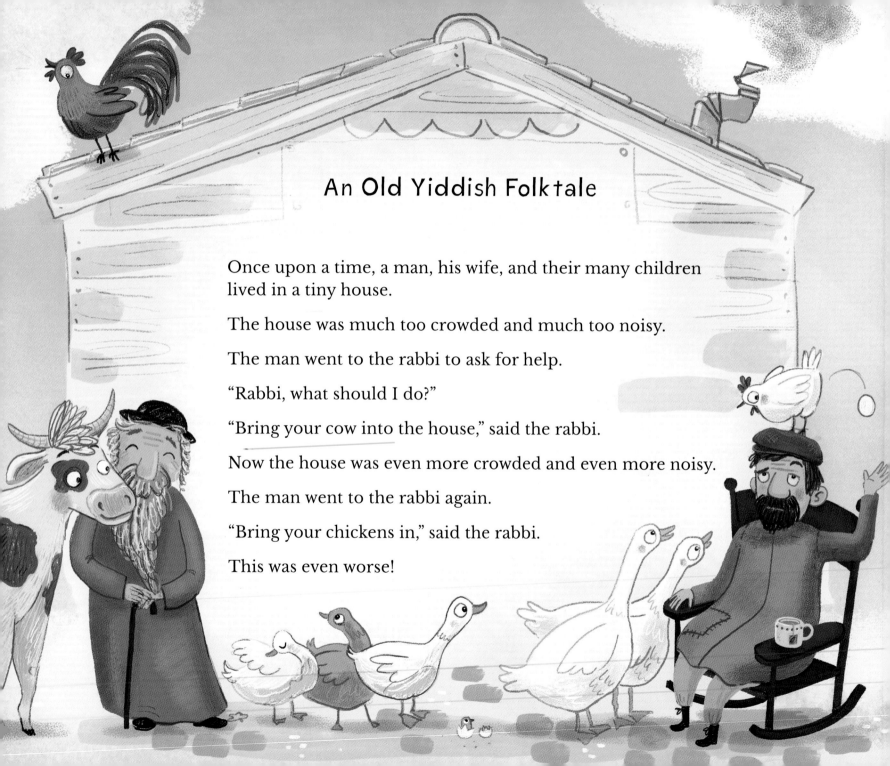

An **Old Yiddish Folktale**

Once upon a time, a man, his wife, and their many children lived in a tiny house.

The house was much too crowded and much too noisy.

The man went to the rabbi to ask for help.

"Rabbi, what should I do?"

"Bring your cow into the house," said the rabbi.

Now the house was even more crowded and even more noisy.

The man went to the rabbi again.

"Bring your chickens in," said the rabbi.

This was even worse!

The man went back to the rabbi.

"Now bring your goats and your geese and your ducks inside," the rabbi told him.

"Rabbi, I can't take it anymore! Please help!"

So the rabbi told the man, "Take out your cow and your chickens and your goats and your geese and your ducks."

And the man did.

Ahh, quiet!

Such a big and spacious house!

For Kenny.
Thank you for running
away from the circus and
joining a home.
—J.R.N.

Text copyright © 2020 by Jill Ross Nadler
Jacket art and interior illustrations © 2020 by Esther van den Berg

Intergalactic Afikoman
1037 NE 65th Street, #167
Seattle, WA 98115

www.IntergalacticAfikoman.com

Publisher's Cataloging-In-Publication Data

Names: Nadler, Jill Ross, author. | Berg, Esther van den, 1982- illustrator.
Title: Such a library! : a Yiddish folktale re-imagined / words by Jill Ross Nadler ; pictures by Esther van den Berg.
Description: First edition. | Seattle : Intergalactic Afikoman, [2020] | Based on the folktale, It could always be worse. | Interest age level: 003-008. | Summary: "Stevie craves quiet until he meets Miss Understood, a magical librarian whose books come to life and wreak havoc, in this modern day twist on an old Yiddish folktale"--Provided by publisher.
Identifiers: ISBN 9781951365028 | ISBN 9781951365035 (ebook)
Subjects: LCSH: Order--Juvenile fiction. | Librarians--Juvenile fiction. | Books--Juvenile fiction. | Magic--Juvenile fiction. | Folk literature, Yiddish. | CYAC: Order--Fiction. | Librarians--Fiction. | Books--Fiction. | Magic--Fiction. | LCGFT: Fantasy fiction.
Classification: LCC PZ8.1.N34 Su 2020 (print) | LCC PZ8.1.N34 (ebook) | DDC [E]--dc23

Library of Congress Control Number: 2020930905

Printed in the USA

First Edition

2 4 6 8 10 9 7 5 3 1

SUCH A LIBRARY!

❧ A Yiddish Folktale Re-imagined ❧

Words by
JILL ROSS NADLER

Pictures by
ESTHER VAN DEN BERG

INTERGALACTIC
Afikoman
SEATTLE

Stevie sat in a big comfy chair in the corner of the Whisper Oaks Public Library.

Ah, quiet.

With three brothers, two sisters, and a baby at home, Stevie's house was never quiet.

But as Stevie opened his book,
he heard pages turning,
whoosh swoosh,
computer keys tapping,
clack click,
and the storyteller saying,
"Once upon a time."

"This library is too noisy," said Stevie.
He tiptoed to the librarian, Miss Understood.

"Excuse me," Stevie whispered.
"Pages are turning,
keys are tapping,
and the storyteller
is once upon a timing.
It's like a party in here."

"A party?" said Miss Understood. "Wonderful idea!" She opened a book. Hundreds of colorful balloons flew from the pages, followed by children with party hats and horns.

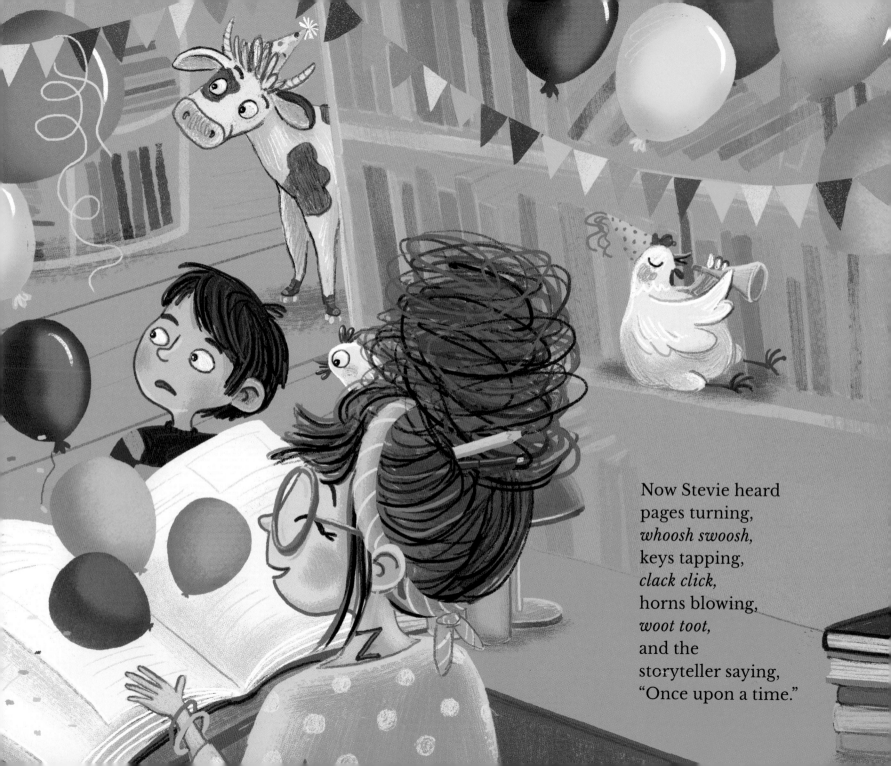

Now Stevie heard
pages turning,
whoosh swoosh,
keys tapping,
clack click,
horns blowing,
woot toot,
and the
storyteller saying,
"Once upon a time."

"Excuse me,"
Stevie said a tiny bit louder.
"Yes?" said Miss Understood.

"Well," said Stevie, "this library is turning into a zoo."

"Outstanding idea!" Miss Understood opened the book and two monkeys, three snakes, a seal, and a kangaroo climbed, slithered, flopped, and hopped out onto the floor.

Now Stevie heard
pages turning,
whoosh swoosh,
keys tapping,
clack click,
horns blowing,
woot toot,
monkeys screeching,
oooh eeee,
and the storyteller saying,
"Once upon a time."

"Excuse me!"

said Stevie even louder this time.

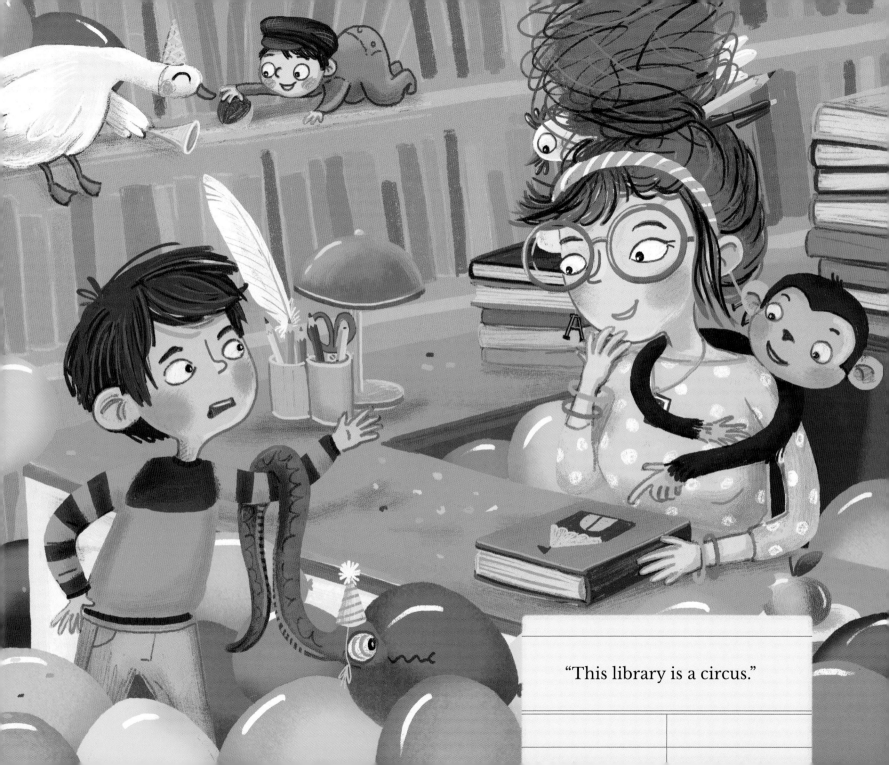

"This library is a circus."

"Stupendous idea!"
Miss Understood opened the book.

Stevie groaned as
an acrobat cartwheeled out,
along with two jugglers,
a ringmaster,
a trapeze artist,
and a tiny car stuffed
with clowns.

Now Stevie heard
pages turning,
whoosh swoosh,
keys tapping,
clack click,
horns blowing,
woot toot,
monkeys screeching,
oooh eeee,
clowns beeping,
ah-ooo gah,
and the storyteller saying,
"Once upon a time."

Stevie couldn't take it anymore.

"EXCUSE ME!"

he shouted.

Miss Understood looked up.

"Oh, Stevie. I didn't hear you with all the pages turning, keys tapping, horns tooting, monkeys screeching, clowns beeping, and the storyteller once upon a timing."

"That's what I've been trying to tell you," Stevie yelled. "This library is too noisy!"

Miss Understood frowned.

"Now, Stevie, there's no need to shout. This is a library after all." She opened the book.

The children,
balloons,
monkeys,
seal,
kangaroo,
snakes,
acrobat,
jugglers,
ringmaster,
trapeze artist,
and clowns,

marched,
flew,
climbed,
flopped,
hopped,
slithered,
cartwheeled,
juggled,
stepped,
swung,
and zoomed back to
their pages.

She handed the book to Stevie.
He took it to his chair and sat down.

As he read,
he heard pages turning,
whoosh swoosh,
computer keys tapping,
clack click,
and the storyteller saying,
"Once upon a time."

Stevie smiled. Ahh, quiet.

And the storyteller said, "The end."

AN OLD YIDDISH FOLKTALE AND ITS RE-IMAGINING

The tale of the man and his crowded house is both completely universal and distinctly Jewish. On the one hand, everyone can identify with the man's problem and the rabbi's clever solution. On the other hand, it is a Yiddish folktale that emerged from life in the shtetl.

But the Jewishness of the original folktale goes far beyond its shtetl setting. As it says in Pirkei Avot, ethical teachings from the rabbis:

אֵיזֶהוּ עָשִׁיר, הַשָּׂמֵחַ בְּחֶלְקוֹ

"Who is rich? The one who is happy with what he has."

This simple and powerful message is the essence of the tale.

Yet the Jewishness of the tale goes still further. In fact, it extends to the story's very approach to life. "Nu? It could be worse," one can almost hear an old Bubbe saying.

But then comes this re-imagining. Is it still a Jewish folktale, one might ask, now that it is no longer set in the shtetl?

Like the Jews have traveled, so have our stories. From the Torah at Sinai to the Talmud in Babylonia. And now from the shtetl in Poland to the Whisper Oaks Public Library in America. As today's Jewish children have traveled, our folktales can travel too.

And if you look closely, you can see that a bit of the shtetl has traveled with them.

JILL ROSS NADLER is the co-founder of Page Turner Adventures, a touring theater company that inspires kids to collect, tell, and write stories. She's written leveled readers for Fountas & Pinnell and a middle-grade novel about a girl who visits strange roadside attractions. In addition to stories, Jill collects names. She's been known as both Riley Roam and Storyologist, Page Turner. She lives in South Florida with her husband and way too many cats.

ESTHER VAN DEN BERG grew up in a Dutch village where she spent her childhood reading books, building huts, and drawing the things that surrounded her. Her love for creating got her into art school. Since graduating as an illustrator, many of her illustrations have found their way into the world. Esther also writes and illustrates her own picture books. She likes to draw animals and humans alike and especially loves how they often resemble each other in their quirky ways. She lives in the Netherlands with her partner and two daughters.